THE CANADA
GOSLINGS

Lilly and Scooter

"A Lesson Learned"

Patricia A. Thorpe

10/23/18

Printed in the United States of America

Revised Date: 03/2018

Library of Congress Control Number: 2018939273

ISBN: Softcover   978-1-948304-64-1

               ePub   978-1-948304-65-8

To order copies of this book, contact:

PageTurner, Press and Media

601 E., Palomar St., Suite C-478 Chula Vista, CA 91911

Phone: 1-888-447-9651

Fax: 1-619-632-6328

Email: order@pageturner.us

www.pageturner.us

Dedication

To my best friend, Lorraine Thorpe. Lorraine was not only my best friend but also like a mother to me. I will always be very grateful to her for the wonderful times we spent together.

Maude and Arnold, Canadian geese, arrived in Wisconsin early in March. They rested for a couple of days after their long trip to a warmer climate and then looked for a nice spot to build a nest for Maude to lay her eggs. Maude and Arnold had raised several different families in Wisconsin for many years in the same area, which was a very comfortable and safe place to build a nest on the shores of Lake Kristine.

Maude and Arnold found the perfect spot to build their nest. They both worked together to build the bowl-shaped nest in a very secluded spot within the cattails and bulrush marshes on the lake's edge. After Maude and Arnold made their finishing touches on the nest, Maude took her place in the nest to start laying her eggs. Arnold stood guard to ensure their new nest and Maude were protected.

Maude laid seven eggs over the next week. She would only leave the nest to find food. Maude knew she must stay healthy to be able to sit on her nest for the next twenty-five to thirty days in order to keep her eggs warm until they hatched. Maude sat on her nest through all different types of weather elements, whether the rain poured down on her or the wind almost blew her off her nest, she stayed on her nest to keep her eggs warm. Then almost thirty days after she laid her eggs, the miracle started to happen as the eggs hatched one by one. Every minute of the day and night, Arnold stood guard over Maude and their nest.

Within twenty-four hours after the eggs hatched into fluffy little goslings, they would be taught to walk, swim, and feed. Arnold will help Maude raise the goslings until their adulthood. The young goslings will remain with their parents for about a year. After the goslings learned to walk, swim, and feed, the goslings' parents must prepare themselves to fly again in fall after what is called "molting." This process runs from June to July in which the adult geese rid themselves of old and worn feathers and replace them with new ones.

After the goslings were about ten weeks old, and the molting season was over, Maude and Arnold were then prepared to teach the young goslings how to fly. This lesson is extremely important. The young goslings must be able to fly with their parents to other places around the area to find food and to a warmer climate as the weather becomes colder. The goslings would not survive without their parents in Wisconsin alone during the cold winter.

L illy and Scooter, two of Maude and Arnold's goslings, had become great friends who learned to walk, swim, and feed together. They played in the lake together along with their other brothers and sisters. But then it was time to learn to fly. The goslings will have to learn how to take off from the water and land on the water while flying from midair. This is the most import thing they will have to learn.

Every afternoon, Maude would give her goslings a signal by moving her neck in a certain way that would indicate it was now time to stop playing and get serious about learning how to fly. Arnold would help gather the goslings in for the training session. This kind of training would take place every day for several weeks. One by one the goslings would learn to scoot across the top of the water and eventually take off into midair and then land on the water again.

All seven goslings were trying in earnest to learn the task of flying. Lilly was one of the first goslings to learn how to take off from the water and land on the water from midair. However, Scooter, one of her brothers had not yet accomplished this difficult task no matter how hard he tried. Maude and Arnold tried to show Scooter what he had to learn as well. Scooter would try over and over again with Lilly, encouraging him by shouting, "Come on, Scooter, you can do it, try harder." But Scooter just wasn't able to do what all his brothers and sisters had accomplished. Maude and Arnold were getting a little worried about Scooter because he wasn't taking learning how to fly very seriously. He just wanted to play with his brothers and sisters. They wanted to test all their goslings very soon by flying to other places around the area to find nourishing food. However, Scooter had to learn to fly!

One day, Lilly decided to talk with Scooter about learning how to fly. Scooter told Lilly, "But I'm afraid that I would never be able to learn to fly." Lilly looked Scooter right in the eye and told him, "Scooter, you're a goose! All geese can learn to fly. You must believe in yourself, Scooter, and keep trying with all your might. I will help you!" "All right, I will try again if you will help me." Scooter told Lilly. So both Lilly and Scooter walked over to the water with Maude and Arnold watching from afar. "Okay Scooter, here is the way I learned to fly." Lilly showed Scooter over and over again how to take off from the water into midair and land on the water from midair. Lilly said, "Now it's your turn, Scooter. Get serious! I know you can do it."

Scooter tried several times to do what Lilly had shown him, but he just could not get off the water into midair. Lilly told Scooter, "Try harder, Scooter, I know you can do it." Scooter swam over to a calm area of the lake, and this time, he told himself, "I know I can do it, I know I can do it." Scooter started flapping his wings harder and harder, and then Scooter was flying in midair. He could hear Lilly shouting, "I knew you could do it Scooter! I knew you could learn to fly!"

17

However, while Scooter was now flying in midair, he knew he would have to learn to land on the water without injuring himself. Scooter said to himself, "It's now or never. I can't fly around in midair forever." Scooter started his descent to the water and landed with a big splash. "Scooter are you all right?" Lilly asked. "Yes, I'm just fine," Scooter told Lilly happily. "I'm just so happy that I finally accomplished my goal of learning how to fly." Scooter not only learned to fly but also learned a great lesson. That lesson was that he could really accomplish any goal by believing in himself and trying very hard by never giving up.

All of a sudden Scooter's sisters and brothers were swimming around Scooter, congratulating him. Maude and Arnold told Scooter how proud they were of him for never giving up. Now they all could fly to other areas around Lake Kristine to find other good, nourishing food. Lilly and Scooter would fly together with the rest of the family wherever they went. Lilly told Scooter, "I think we all learned a great lesson."

"Never give up and just keep trying!"

CPSIA information can be obtained
at www.ICGtesting.com
Printed in the USA
LVHW07n2251111018
593319LV00002B/6/P